THE ONCE UPON A TIME MAP BOOK

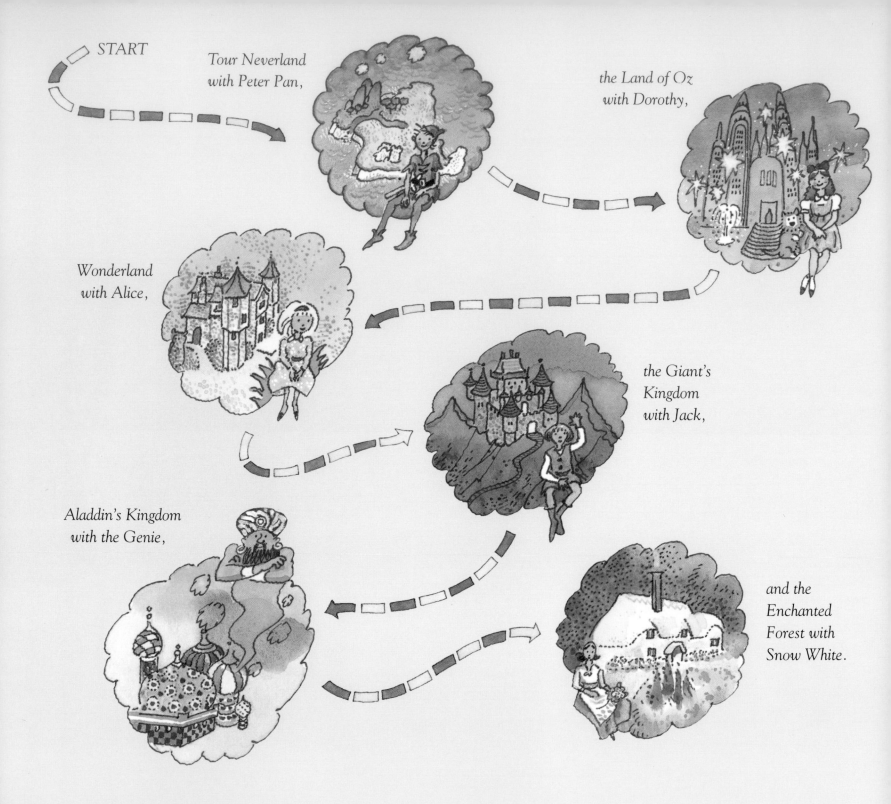

START

Tour Neverland with Peter Pan,

the Land of Oz with Dorothy,

Wonderland with Alice,

the Giant's Kingdom with Jack,

Aladdin's Kingdom with the Genie,

and the Enchanted Forest with Snow White.

Enjoy the trip!

THE ONCE UPON A TIME MAP BOOK

Come on a tour of six magical
Once Upon a Time lands.

You will have a map and directions for
each land. Around each map are letters
and numbers to help you find your way.
A compass shows the directions of
north, south, east, and west. A key
identifies local routes and distances.

There are treasures hidden in each land.
See if you can find all six.

B. G. HENNESSY

illustrated by

PETER JOYCE

CANDLEWICK PRESS
CAMBRIDGE, MASSACHUSETTS

PETER PAN AND TINKERBELL'S TOUR OF
NEVERLAND

Join Peter Pan and Tinkerbell to begin your tour of Neverland. Travel through jungles, swamps, and mountains, along creeks, and through treacherous swamps. Peter and Tink have hidden a magical treasure chest filled with pixie dust somewhere along the way. See if you can find it!

POINTS OF INTEREST

THE JOLLY ROGER
A handsome ship for some dastardly pirates, now anchored in Pirate's Cove.

WENDY'S HOUSE
The original cottage built for Wendy by Peter and the Lost Boys.

PETER'S HIDEOUT
Most of it is underground and unknown to Hook and his crew.

DANGER

Watch out for crocodiles — especially ones that tick!

Stay away from pirates!

tick
tick

MERMAID COVE

CROCODILE SWAMP

tick

PIRATE RIVER

TIGER LILY LAGOON

NEVERLAND

- Moor your boat at Mermaid Cove (E1).
- Take the sandy path east. Where the path splits go south through the jungle.
- At Crocodile Swamp follow the path east. Go around the swamp and use the stepping stones to cross the bog at Pirate River (E3).
- Go 2 Pirate miles west on the rock path. Then follow it behind the waterfall (D3).
- Head southeast on the rock path. At the twin trees take the war path until it ends at the Indian camp (D5).
- Go west 6 Pirate miles. At the rock that looks like a duck, take the coastal path north toward Pirate Village.
- Continue northwest around Pirate's Cove and cross Hook's Creek on the gangplank.
- Follow the bank upstream to the rope bridge. Then cross the creek again.
- Peter Pan and Tinkerbell will take you to Peter's hideout and then north to Wendy's house.

Did you find the treasure chest?

The seven Lost Boys are hiding. How many can you find?

KEY

2 PIRATE MILES

SANDY PATH

ROCK PATH

WAR PATH

COASTAL PATH

DOROTHY'S TOUR OF
THE LAND OF OZ

Join Dorothy and her friends for a tour of the magical Land of Oz. Stop to visit Munchkin Land on your way to the Emerald City. The Great Oz will be waiting to take you up in his hot-air balloon. Don't forget to look for the treasure—two emerald-and-gold crowns.

POINTS OF INTEREST

MUNCHKIN HOUSES
Everything is made to Munchkin size.

PALACE OF OZ
The sparkling centerpiece of the Emerald City.

DANGER
Keep your eyes open for nasty flying monkeys.

Stay clear of the poppy field.

Watch out for those pesky cyclones!

CHINA LANDS

WICKED WITCH CASTLE RUINS

GLINDA'S CASTLE

Column labels (top): D E F G H

Row labels (right side): 1 2 3 4 5

THE LAND OF OZ

- The tour starts at Dorothy's house (H4).
- Go southwest 2 Munchkin miles on the dirt road. The Yellow Brick Road begins at the polka-dot Munchkin houses.
- Follow the Yellow Brick Road through Munchkin Land and the Great Forest to the brick bridge (D3).
- Take the rowboat moored under the brick bridge. Row 11 Munchkin miles upstream, passing the Poppy Field.
- Moor the boat at the turret bridge (C2) just beyond the tree that looks like a witch. Head northeast 3 Munchkin miles on the pebble path back to the Yellow Brick Road. Go west to the Emerald City.
- The Great Oz will meet you at the east gate (D1) for a tour of the city. After lunch, he'll take you on a balloon ride. The balloon is tethered at the west gate.
- Float southwest over the Forest of Fighting Trees. Then float east to the center of the China Lands (B3).
- The Good Witch of the South's castle is due south. Glinda will be waiting.

Did you find the crowns?

Can you find the 6 buckets of water Dorothy has hidden in case the Wicked Witch of the West shows up?

EMERALD CITY

POPPY FIELD

MUNCHKIN LAND

KEY

1 MUNCHKIN MILE

YELLOW BRICK ROAD

PEBBLE PATH

DIRT ROAD

Column labels (bottom): D E F G H

ALICE'S TOUR OF
WONDERLAND

Look for Alice near the Rabbit Hole. She's hoping to see her friends the Cheshire Cat and the White Rabbit on this tour. Because Wonderland is always changing, even Alice isn't quite sure what you'll find or where you'll be when you get there. Now where *did* she hide the tea set?

POINTS OF INTEREST

THE DUCHESS'S HOUSE
It looks orderly only from the outside.

THE CROQUET GROUND
Full of bumps and holes — a most difficult place to play.

THE RABBIT HOLE
Examine the walls on your way down.

DANGER
Don't eat anything! Food in Wonderland has some very strange side effects.

Eat me.

Drink me.

CROQUET GROUND

Grid labels

D   E   F   G   H

1   2   3   4   5

DUCHESS'S HOUSE

EL OF TREES

ROSE GARDEN

MAZE GARDEN

HALL OF LAMPS

KEY

50 WHITE RABBIT HOPS

Brick Path

Zigzag Path

Gravel Path

WONDERLAND

- The tour will begin at the Rabbit Hole (H1). Go down. And down. And down.
- At the bottom (H5), turn west into the Hall of Lamps. Go through the smallest door and north into the Maze Garden.
- Find your way through the maze.
- Leave the maze and go west down the steps. Follow the brick path counterclockwise around the fountain. Take the north path and go through the wooden door.
- Follow the zigzag path to the Rose Garden (E3). Circle all the way around it to the bush that looks like a peacock.
- Enter the Tunnel of Trees (E2). At the end, go south under the arch in the hedge to the Croquet Ground.
- Find the 2 of hearts, then the 3, 4, 5, 6, 7, 8, and 9 of hearts. They will lead you to a tree with six branches.
- Go through the small gate next to the tree (A3) and follow the gravel path 250 White Rabbit hops north to the March Hare's house. Enjoy the tea party!

Did you find the tea set?

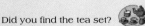

Can you find the Cheshire Cat? He's in four different places.

JACK'S TOUR OF THE
GIANT'S KINGDOM

Jack has planted his last magic bean and grown a new beanstalk. There is no Giant to worry about now, and the views are breathtaking. Jack is waiting at the top, so put on your hiking shoes and start climbing. Somewhere along the way Jack has hidden his special treasure—the Giant's basket of golden eggs.

POINTS OF INTEREST

GIANT'S CASTLE

Walk through the dungeon where the Giant's prisoners were kept. Don't miss a visit to the treasure room.

HURRICANE FALLS

The water has the force of a storm.

RAINBOW BRIDGE

If you are lucky, it will appear. There isn't any other way across Inky Blue River.

DANGER

Watch your step climbing the beanstalk! It sways in the wind.

Be very careful going through Windy Pass.

A   **B**

1

HURRICANE FALLS

2

FUM

3

FOGGY PEAKS

FI

4

INKY BLUE RIVER

SKELETON MESA

5

A   **B**

THE GIANT'S KINGDOM

- From Jack's house (G5), climb the beanstalk to Pile of Bones Road.
- Follow Pile of Bones Road southwest 8 Giant steps to the town of Fee.
- Go west through Fee and cross Inky Blue River on Cloud Bridge (C5).
- Continue west around Skeleton Mesa and go 2 Giant steps northeast past the town of Fi.
- Cross Inky Blue River again on Skull Bridge.
- Follow the rock path around Foggy Peaks. Climb the rock ledge and go across it (C3). Continue east through Boulder Flats.
- Cross Footstep Canyon on the log bridge. Continue on the rock path through the town of Fo and Golden Egg Pass (E3).
- Take the grassy path 4 Giant steps west to Rainbow Bridge (B3). Go across it and take the steps through the town of Fum.
- Climb through Windy Pass and up, up, up the Giant's stairs to the Giant's castle. Relax and enjoy the view.

Did you find the basket of eggs?

Can you find the Giant's hen and golden harp?

KEY

1 GIANT STEP

PILE OF BONES ROAD

ROCK PATH

GRASSY PATH

GIANT'S STAIRS

FO

BOULDER FLATS

FEE

N
NW   NE
W   E
SW   SE
S

The Genie's Tour of
ALADDIN'S KINGDOM

The Genie of the Lamp is ready to take you on a tour of Aladdin's Kingdom. Join him and enjoy the exotic sights—the marketplace, the gardens, the fountains, and the palaces. Perhaps you will find a magic lamp of your own! During your visit, remember to look for Aladdin's magic flying carpet.

POINTS OF INTEREST

ALADDIN'S PALACE
Considered by many to be the finest palace in the world.

CAVE OF TREASURES
The halls are filled with gold, silver, and jewels.

WATER WELL AND WISHING WELL
Make sure you know the difference, or your wish may not come true!

WATER WELL

WISHING WELL

DANGER

Watch out for the Evil Magician. Trust no one!

Don't touch anything in the Cave of Treasures, or it will collapse around *you!*

ALADDIN'S   PALA

SULTAN'S PALACE

A   B

1
2
3
4
5

A   B

TWIN MOUNTAINS

ALADDIN'S KINGDOM

- Tie up your camel outside the gates (H5).
- Go west through the gates. At the water well (E5), turn north and climb two flights of steps to the Fountain of Elephants (E3).
- Go counterclockwise around the Fountain and turn southwest down the Street of Palms. Go under the blue-tiled archway (D4) and walk south to the wishing well (D5)
- At the wishing well, take 20 Genie steps west. Turn north and go under the purple leopard archway and into Merchants' Marketplace.
- Walk west past the carpet seller and climb the golden steps to the grounds of the Sultan's palace (B4).
- Leave through the door in the north wall. Follow the red carpet (B3) 43 Genie steps to Aladdin's Palace.
- After a tour of the palace, picnic in the gardens with Aladdin and the Genie.
- Leave the gardens through the east gate. Turn north on Camel Road (F2).
- Aladdin and the Genie will take you beyond Twin Mountains to the Cave of Treasures.

Did you find the flying carpet?

Can you find Ali Baba . . . and his forty thieves?

KEY

10 GENIE STEPS

STREET OF PALMS

RED CARPET

CAMEL ROAD

SNOW WHITE AND THE SEVEN DWARFS' TOUR OF

THE ENCHANTED FOREST

The Enchanted Forest is the last stop on your trip. With Snow White and the Seven Dwarfs, scale the Jewel Hills for a panoramic view of Mirror Lake and the Evil Queen's orchard. The dwarfs have decorated a beautiful mirror with jewels from their mines. Can you find it?

POINTS OF INTEREST

DWARFS' COTTAGE
There are seven of everything — the playhouse you've always wanted!

JEWEL MINES
Don't miss the seven mines — gold, silver, copper, ruby, diamond, emerald, and sapphire.

DANGER
Don't eat any apples — no matter how delicious they look.

RUBY HILL

SAPPHIRE HILL

EM

ENCHANTED PALACE

ROYAL HUNTING GROUNDS

A   B

1

2

3

4

5

DIAMOND HILL

...HILL

COPPER HILL

SILVER HILL

GOLD HILL

MIRROR LAKE

THE ENCHANTED FOREST

- Snow White will meet you at the palace gates (A3).
- Head south through the Royal Hunting Grounds.
  At the stables, take the hunter's path east to the stone wall.
- Follow the stone wall north 2 Dwarf miles to the wooden gate.
- The Seven Dwarfs will meet you there and help you find your
  way north through the bramble thicket.
- At the end of the thicket, take the dirt path 2 Dwarf miles to
  the huntsman's hut (C3).
- Follow the dirt path west and climb Sapphire Hill. Cross the
  hanging bridge to Ruby Hill. Go around Ruby Hill and continue
  east, crossing the Jewel Hills on the hanging bridges until you
  reach Gold Hill (F2).
- Take the miner's trail down toward Mirror Lake.
  DO NOT GO OVER THE STONE BRIDGE. This part of the forest
  is still under an evil spell. Head west and walk counterclockwise
  around the lake, passing the Evil Queen's apple orchard.
- At the circle of trees, enter the Deep, Dark Forest (D4). Follow the
  winding stream to the wooden footbridge (E5).
- Cross the wooden footbridge and climb up to the Dwarfs' cottage.

Did you find the mirror?

Can you find the basket of poisoned apples dropped by the Evil Queen?

Your tour of the Lands of Once Upon a Time is over.
Hop on the Royal Coach for the trip home,
where everyone lives happily ever after!

KEY

2 DWARF MILES

HUNTER'S PATH

DIRT PATH

MINER'S TRAIL

WINDING STREAM

Text copyright © 1999 by B. G. Hennessy
Illustrations copyright © 1999 by Peter Joyce

All rights reserved.

Second edition 2004

Library of Congress Cataloging-in-Publication Data is available.

Library of Congress Catalog Card Number 98-72608

ISBN 0-7636-2521-3

2 4 6 8 10 9 7 5 3 1

Printed in China

Candlewick Press
2067 Massachusetts Avenue
Cambridge, Massachusetts 02140

visit us at www.candlewick.com